WITHDRAWN

JACK RUSSELL:
Dog Detective

WITHDRAWN

The Ham Heist

JACK RUSSELL: Dog Detective

JACK RUSSELL: Dog Detective

The Ham Heist

DARREL & SALLY ODGERS

Kane Miller

A DIVISION OF EDC PUBLISHING

First American Edition 2010
by Kane Miller, A Division of EDC Publishing

First published by Scholastic Australia in 2010.
Cover copyright © Lake Shore Graphics, 2010.
Photo of dog, Frisbee, courtesy of the Cansick family.
Photo of puppy, Preacher, courtesy of Darrel and Sally Odgers.
Illustrations copyright © Scholastic Australia, 2010.
Illustrations by Janine Dawson.

For information contact:
Kane Miller, A Division of EDC Publishing
P.O. Box 470663
Tulsa, OK 74147-0663
www.kanemiller.com
www.edcpub.com

Library of Congress Control Number: 2009943490

Printed and bound in the United States of America
1 2 3 4 5 6 7 8 9 10
ISBN: 978-1-935279-75-4

For Ace, 10/08/2001 to 13/02/2006,
our inspiration for this series.

–Darrel and Sally Odgers

To Pippi, the artist's muse.

–Janine Dawson

Dear Readers,

The story you're about to
read is about me and my friends,
and how we solved The Case of the Ham
Heist. To save time, I'll introduce us all to
you now. If you know us already, trot off to
Chapter One.

I am Jack Russell, Dog Detective. I live
with my landlord, Sarge, in Doggeroo. Sarge
detects human-type crimes. I have the
important job of detecting crimes that deal
with dogs. I'm a Jack Russell terrier, so I am
dogged and intelligent. Preacher lives with
us. He is a clever, handsome junior Jack
Russell. His mother is my friend Jill Russell.

Next door to Sarge and me live Auntie
Tidge and Foxie. Auntie Tidge is lovely. She
has biscuits and fowls. Foxie is not lovely.
He's a fox terrier (more or less). He used to

be a street dog and a thief, but he's reformed now. Auntie Tidge has even gotten rid of his fleas. Foxie sometimes helps me with my cases.

Uptown Lord Setter (Lord Red for short) lives in Uptown House with Caterina Smith. Lord Red means well, but he isn't very bright. Caterina and Sarge are best friends. Caterina's uncle, Uncle Smith, sometimes visits them.

Other friends and acquaintances in Doggeroo include Polly the dachshund, the Squekes, Ralf Boxer and Shuffle the pug. Then there's Fat Molly, but she's only the cat from the library.

That's all you need to know, so let's get on with Chapter One.

Yours doggedly,

Jack Russell — the detective with a nose for crime.

Waiting For a Case

Preacher and I were watching comings and goings next door when Jill Russell joined us on our porch.

"Mum Russell!" Preacher waggled and grinned.

Jill gave him a quick face wash, then poked me with her nose. She always does that. "My person is helping Auntie Tidge with Sarge and Caterina's wedding feast. Let's go to the park."

It had been a while since we'd had time for fun. Sarge was busy, but after he and Caterina Smith had their wedding feast, we'd all live with Caterina and Lord Red. Red used to be a **pawfully** dim-witted dog, but associating with me had improved his intelligence.

Jack's Facts

Some dogs are intelligent.
Some dogs are dim-witted.
Associating with an intelligent dog makes a dim-witted dog less dim-witted.
This is a fact.

Preacher followed us to our gate. Then he looked down the street to where some children were kicking a ball. "I'll stay here," he said. "Those **dog-boggarts** might get me."

Jill looked at him in astonishment. "Don't be silly, Preacher."

Preacher sat down.

"We'll go without you," I said. Even that didn't move my junior Jack, so we left without him.

"What's this **dogwash** about dog-boggarts?" asked Jill, as we trotted along.

"Since those children frightened Preacher, he thinks that all children are out to get him," I explained.

Jill snorted. "Preacher mustn't be scared of dog-boggarts. He's a Jack Russell terrier. Jacks are bold and brave. Sort it out, Jack."

"How?" I asked.

"Get his mind off it," said Jill. "Get him busy."

Of paws, she was right. I am a dog detective, which is an **im-paw-tant** position. I should help Preacher feel im-paw-tant too.

"He can help solve my next case," I said.

"Get a case now," Jill ordered.

"I can't get a case. Detectives have to wait for a crime before we sniff out criminals."

"Don't be silly, Jack. I'll set up a case for Preacher to solve."

"Like what?" I asked.

"You'll see," said Jill.

Jack's Glossary

Pawfully. *Very, awfully.*

Dog-boggarts. *Small, fast-moving children who grab dogs.*

Dogwash. *Nonsense.*

Of paws. *The same as "of course," but for dogs.*

Im-paw-tant. *Important, for dogs.*

A Whole Huge Ham

After a game at the park, we went home. Just as we got there, the butcher's van pulled up next door. Foxie shot through his **dogdoor** yelling about ham.

"Ham?" Jill Russell looked **interrier-ested**. We terriers know the value of good food.

"Ham! Ham! Mine, mine, mine!" yammered Foxie, prancing around the van.

Of paws, Jill and I scooted next door to investigate. Preacher followed us.

Jack's Facts

A few dogs are dog detectives.
Most dogs are not.
All dogs become detectives when ham
is involved.
This is a fact.

Butcher Beale got out to open the van's back doors. Foxie bounced, yammered and drooled. Preacher waggled and grinned. Jill sniff-sniffed. Even I dribbled a bit.

The back of that van smelled good. My

super-sniffer detected sausages, beef, mutton and ham. I **Jack-yapped**, to let Butcher Beale know I wanted ham. He paid no attention. I **Jack-jumped** to get his attention. Preacher waggled so fast his tail was a blur. Jill sniff-sniffed.

"Ham! Ham!" yelled Foxie. "Mine, mine, mine!"

"Scat!" said Butcher Beale. We didn't, so he got back into his van and leaned on the horn. It made a **terrier-able** noise. Preacher squealed and fled with his tail between his legs. I followed.

We watched from our porch as Auntie Tidge came out. She tutted at Foxie. He was still yammering, so she had to shout to Butcher Beale.

"Thank you, Mr. Beale. I'll take it. *Down* Foxie! Bad dog! *Down!*" Auntie Tidge took the ham. It was huge! The breeze carried ham scent all over Doggeroo.

"*Mine!*" screamed Foxie.

He made so much noise we didn't notice Sarge until he went to help Auntie Tidge.

Just as he reached her, Auntie Tidge tripped over Foxie and dropped the whole huge ham. Of paws, Foxie made a dive for it. Sarge got there first and caught it just before it hit the ground. "Quiet, Foxie!" he yelled. "Are you all right, Auntie?"

"Yes, dear," said Auntie Tidge. She put her glasses straight. "The butcher's van makes Foxie forget his manners."

"I'll take the ham into the kitchen. Shut Foxie in the shed," said Sarge.

He headed for the kitchen, and Auntie Tidge tried to get Foxie into the shed.

Foxie shot under the hedge and scooted

through our dogdoor. Preacher and I followed and found him hiding under Sarge's bed. We crawled in after him. A moment later, our dogdoor clonked, and Jill Russell joined us. "Auntie Tidge used the *shed* word," she said.

"It's unfair," sulked Foxie. "That whole huge ham almost hit the ground."

We all sighed.

Jack's Facts

Good dogs don't steal food.
Food that hits the ground automatically belongs to dogs.
Therefore, it is not stealing to eat food from the floor.
*In fact, it is **salvage**.*
This is a fact.

"I want ham," said Preacher.

"We all want ham," I told my junior Jack. "That doesn't mean we'll get any."

Foxie growled. "That ham was delivered to my house. It is mine by right."

"You won't get your jaws on that ham," I said. "Auntie Tidge will hide it."

"And *I'll* find it and heist it," said Foxie.

Jack's Glossary

Dogdoor. *A door especially for dogs.*

Interrier-ested. *Interested, for terriers.*

Super-sniffer. *Jack's nose in super-tracking mode.*

Jack-yap. *A loud, piercing yap made by a Jack Russell terrier.*

Jack-jump. *A very athletic spring done by a Jack Russell terrier.*

Terrier-able. *Very bad.*

Salvage. *Food that would be wasted if we didn't eat it.*

Paw-tential Pupetrators

Later, Jill, Preacher, Foxie and I crept out to sit on our porch. We watched more comings and goings. I knew most of the people and cars, but one van was strange.

Jill's person called her. "Don't forget that new case!" she told me, as she trotted away.

"What case, Dad?" asked Preacher.

"I can't tell you yet," I said. That was true, because I didn't know yet.

Preacher sniff-sniffed the air. "I'll make a **nose map**, Dad."

Preacher's map:

1. *Whole huge ham.*

2. *Sarge.*

3. *Auntie Tidge.*

4. *Dora Barkins.*

5. *Gloria Smote.*

6. *Strange people in boots.*

7. *Tina Boxer.*

I **verified** Preacher's map with my super-sniffer. "Very good," I said. "The Boot people must have come in the strange van."

"I didn't add everyone who has already gone," said Preacher. He sighed. "My nose map doesn't suggest a case. Unless Uncle Foxie really does heist the huge ham."

Foxie swallowed. "When I get my jaws on that ham I'll eat lots. I'll nibble and lick. I'll chew the rind and feast on the meat. Then, I'll bury the bone in Auntie Tidge's herb garden. I'll dig it up when I feel like another chew. Then I'll–"

Foxie yelped as I bit his tail. "Do you *want* to spend the rest of your life in the shed?" I asked. "Do *not* heist that ham."

"I **sup-paws** you and Jill want to do it," snarled Foxie.

"Is that true, Dad?" Preacher looked worried.

"Of *paws* not," I snapped. I *hoped* not! Although Jill Russell had said she'd set up a case for Preacher.

I had to prevent Jill and Foxie from ham heisting. I'd set up a **doggo obbo** to guard the goods.

"Come," I told my junior Jack. "We'll verify the ham's position. Then we'll know if someone moves in on it." I sniff-sniffed. The ham scent was strong. I knew **sniffers** were working overtime all over Doggeroo. Good dogs were having bad thoughts.

"We'll soon be dogged by **paw-tential pupetrators**," I told Preacher.

"What if there are dog-boggarts?" he asked.

"We're going to Foxie's yard," I reminded him. "There are no dog-boggarts there." We crept under our hedge. Foxie wanted to come, but I reminded him about the shed.

Preacher and I sneaked under a bush to **stake out** the front door.

Soon, Polly Smote and her pup Spotty Sprat arrived, sniff-sniffing the air. The Squekes came next, then Ralf Boxer and Shuffle. My pals had sniffers raised. Pools of drool gathered on the pavement. Even Fat Molly prowled by.

"Molly!" Preacher waggled over to her. Molly whisker-swiped along his face, then

spotted me. She **pussyfooted** away.

Preacher gulped. "Dad, are all those paw-tential pupetrators?"

"They'd like to be," I said. "Jack-yap to disperse them."

Preacher stuck his nose through the gate, then backed away. "You do it, Dad. There might be dog-boggarts."

I left Auntie Tidge's yard (never mind how) and addressed the paw-tential pupetrators. "I know you hope to heist the whole huge ham," I said. "But if you turn into canine criminals, I'll arrest you. Then you'll get shut in the shed and miss getting salvage at the wedding feast at Uptown House. Think about it."

They thought about it.

"Go home!" I commanded. When Jack Russells command, dogs obey. They went.

Jack's Glossary

Nose map. *Way of storing information collected by the nose.*

Verify. *Make sure something is correct.*

Sup-paws. *Suppose, for dogs.*

Doggo obbo. *Official observation, performed by a dog.*

Sniffer. *A dog's nose in tracking mode. Only Jack Russell terriers have super-sniffers.*

Paw-tential pupetrators. *Dogs who might turn out to be canine criminals.*

Stake out. *Hide and watch for pupetrators.*

Pussyfoot. *The way cats walk. Also known as catfooting.*

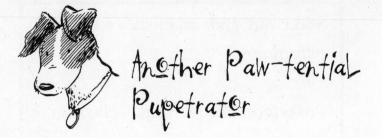

Another Paw-tential Pupetrator

I was back with Preacher when Lord Red sailed over the fence and pounced on me.

"Hello, Jack! Hello, Preacher! Guess what? Kiarna, Uncle Smith, Blue and—yow! Why are you swinging on my ear, Jack?"

"You pounced on me," I said, spitting out stray hairs.

Jack's Facts

If small dogs don't defend themselves, big dogs take advantage. Therefore, small dogs must defend themselves. This is a fact.

"Sorry, Jack. I'm pawfully excited," said Red. "Kiarna and Uncle Smith and–"

"You said that before," I reminded him.

"Who's Kiarna?" asked Preacher.

"Kiarna's lovely. She has treats. She plays hide-and-squeak. She's my almost-best person," said Red. "She'll help Caterina Smith carry flowers at the wedding feast. But–" Suddenly Red stiffened his tail and **pointed**. "I smell *ham!*"

"Yes," I said. "You're the last dog in Doggeroo to notice it."

"Auntie Tidge has a whole huge ham for the wedding feast," put in Preacher. "We're guarding it from paw-tential pupetrators."

"I'll help." Red licked his chops. "But shouldn't we be closer in case Foxie gets it?"

"Foxie's at our place," I said.

"He might have nipped back for a

nibble," said Red.

That made sense. Preacher and I went in through Foxie's dogdoor. Lord Red bolted through and ouched his tail. He spun in circles, yelping.

This made a **pawfect dog-straction** while Preacher and I sniff-sniffed around the crowded kitchen. We tracked the ham to the pantry, but the door was closed, and it had a round handle.

Jack's Facts

Jacks are nimble. Jacks are smart.
Not even a Jack can turn a round handle.
Therefore, all handles should be long ones.
This is a fact.

Preacher pointed at the pantry. "The

ham's in there, Dad." He sniff-sniffed the edge of the door. "There are lots of things. I detect cake, and cheese, and pies."

We jumped back as Auntie Tidge opened the pantry door. She shooed us away gently with her foot. "Everything on these two shelves is to go in your van tomorrow, along with the chairs," she said to someone behind us. "It will take two trips." Out of the corner of my eye I saw a big brown boot much too

close to my tail. I sniff-sniffed. It belonged to one of the strangers Preacher had nose-mapped.

"Fine, **Miss Russell**," said Brown Boots. I twitched my tail out of the way just in time.

Auntie Tidge shooed me again. "Do you need directions to Uptown House?"

"We know where it is. We put up a greenhouse there a few weeks ago, and we're doing the tent for the wedding," said Brown Boots. "That's a fine ham! Look, boys!"

Another two pairs of boots crowded in behind us. One pair was old. The other was new and shiny and smelled of something that was not leather. Old Boots whistled. "That's the biggest ham I've ever seen. Smells good."

"My mum won't buy ham," said Shiny Boots. "She's a **vegetarian**. It's not fair. I love ham." He was using **humanspeak**, of paws, but he reminded me of Foxie when he was sulking.

"Do we take the ham in the van, Miss Russell?" asked Old Boots.

"No, I'll take that myself with the wedding cake, last thing," said Auntie Tidge. "Excuse me, someone's at the door." She closed the pantry and bustled towards the front door. Lord Red dashed ahead of her.

"It's Uncle Smith and Kiarna!" Red launched at the door. The dogdoor clonked, but Red scrabbled the handle with his front paws. "Kiarna! Kiarna! Play with meeeee!"

Auntie Tidge pushed Red away and opened the door. Brown Boots, Old Boots and Shiny Boots tramped out. Shiny Boots was still grumbling about his mum and her eating habits.

Dora Barkins, Tina Boxer and Gloria Smote said goodbye and followed them out.

Next, Uncle Smith came in. I **greeted** him.

"Hello, Jack Russell!" He put me down and shook hands with Sarge. "I'll put Red out before he knocks the door down." He **collared** Red and put him out, then sniffed the air. "Something smells good."

"It's this ham." Sarge opened the pantry. A waft of ham scent made my mouth water.

"My *word*, that's the biggest ham I've ever seen!" said Uncle Smith.

"Yes, dear," said Auntie Tidge. "There's a saddle of beef too, and a whole salmon."

I saw Preacher edging back towards the pantry, but loud sniff-sniffing from outside Foxie's dogdoor dog-stracted me. I was about to go out and investigate when the dog came in. He **pawsed** when he saw me.

I Jack-jumped in front of him. "Stop, in the

name of the paw!" This dog was another paw-tential pupetrator, and I had arrested him before. It was the blue stealer!

Jack's Glossary

Pointed. *Clever dogs use their noses to point to things.*

Pawfect. *Perfect, but about dogs.*

Dog-straction. *A distraction made by a dog.*

Miss Russell. *I am Jack Russell. Sarge is Sergeant Russell. Auntie Tidge is Miss Russell.*

Vegetarian. *A person or animal who doesn't eat meat. Dogs are not naturally vegetarians.*

Humanspeak. *The not-so-private speech of humans. Clever dogs can understand it.*

Greeted. *This is done by rising to the hind legs and clutching a person with the paws while slurping them up the face.*

Collared. *Grabbed by the collar.*

Pawsed. *Stopped to think with paw upraised.*

Kiarna

"I'm not making trouble, Jack Russell," said the blue stealer.

"You did the last time you were in Doggeroo!" I reminded him.

The blue stealer sat down. "I was bad then," he said. "I'm a good dog now. Uncle Smith is my new pack's **alpha**. Barley and little Painter are in my new pack, and we're all good dogs."

Blue *did* look different. He wasn't as thin, and his coat shone. But I'd heard him sniffing. I knew what that meant. "You were sniff-sniffing that whole huge ham."

"Of paws!" said Blue. "So were you and the junior Jack."

I **ig-gnawed** that. "Can you deny you plan to heist that ham?"

Blue licked his chops. "I won't heist the ham. That fox terrier out there is the one singing a ham heisting song."

I pricked up my ears. Blue was right. I detected a high-pitched whine coming from outside the door. "That's Foxie," I said. "You remember him. This is his **terrier-tory**."

"Then that ham is his by right," said Blue. "Back off, Jack Russell."

I started to hackle, then thought better of it. Jacks are brave, but fighting a blue heeler is a bad idea. Besides, if Blue was a good dog now, it would be bad to turn him back into a bad dog. To dog-stract him, I cocked my head.

As I did that, I realized Foxie's song had stopped. I ducked past Blue and left by the dogdoor. It clonked as he followed.

Foxie was rushing across his yard, yapping. Red galloped after him. Of paws, I dashed off in **pawsuit**.

<u>Jack's Facts</u>

Jack Russells are terriers.
Terriers are chasing dogs as well as
digging dogs.
Therefore, when something runs, it is only
natural for Jacks to run after it.
This is a fact.

Foxie shot back past me. Then Blue tore behind the house, sending Auntie Tidge's hens into **hen-sterics**.

Foxie and Red followed, and so did I. Preacher caught up as we changed direction again. "Dad? What's the **pan-dog-monium**?"

"I'm trying to find out," I said. We all galloped back past the hens, then Red and Blue dived into some bushes after Foxie.

Red pranced around, barking. "Kiarna! Kiarna! Scratch meeee!"

I heard a giggle. "All *right*, Lordie."

Lordie is what Caterina Smith calls Lord Red. But the voice wasn't Caterina's. I pawsed and sniff-sniffed.

Preacher bounced past me, yapping at Foxie. Suddenly he squealed and shot back out with his tail clamped between his legs. A few seconds later I heard our dogdoor clonk as my junior Jack escaped to hide under Sarge's bed.

I dived into the bushes, yapping.

Red bounced out. "What's wrong?"

"Halt in the name of the paw!" I ordered. Red stopped, and I **interrier-gated** him. "Who attacked Preacher? Was it Blue?"

"Who? What? Of paws not!" Red sounded puzzled. "Blue's good now. He doesn't—"

"Was it the person in the bushes?" I asked.

"Don't be silly, Jack. That's Kiarna. Kiarna's lovely. She has treats. She—"

I lost interest in the interrier-gation then because Kiarna crawled out of the bushes. She had Foxie snuggled under her chin. My pal was wagging his tail, squirming like a pup.

Kiarna plopped down on the grass. Red and Blue dived at her and tried to get their noses into her pocket. She giggled again and gave them treats. Then she saw me. "Oh, you must be Jack!" she said. She rubbed my head. I found myself wagging my tail and grinning as foolishly as Foxie. I saw why Kiarna was one of Red's best people. Like all my best people, she really, *really* liked dogs.

I also saw why my junior Jack had been so **terrier-fied**. Kiarna knew all the best games, but she was also a small, fast-moving human. Kiarna looked like a dog-boggart.

"Red!" I Jack-jumped to get his attention. "Kiarna is pawfect for Preacher."

Red sat down and cocked his head to one side. "She is?"

"She *looks* like a dog-boggart, but she doesn't *act* like one," I explained. "We have to introduce her to Preacher to show him not all children are dog-boggarts."

I scooted back to our place and crawled under the bed with Preacher. "Come along," I said sternly. "Help me guard that ham."

"There's a *dog-boggart* in Uncle Foxie's

yard," whined Preacher.

"There's no dog-boggart in Foxie's yard," I promised. This was true. Kiarna wasn't a dog-boggart.

Preacher crept out and slunk after me. Looking **hangdog,** he followed me under the hedge. Red galloped up and bounced to a stop, blocking the hole we'd just crawled through. Kiarna, Foxie and Blue dashed after him.

Preacher cowered.

Kiarna flopped down when she saw him. "Oh, hello," she said softly, and held out her hand. "Did I scare you?" She turned to the rest of us. "Shhhh . . . settle down now."

Foxie crawled into Kiarna's lap and squirmed as she scratched his chest. Red and Blue lay down and rested their chins on her legs.

Preacher whined. "Preacher," I said
sternly. "Stop. Kiarna *likes* you."

Kiarna took a treat from her pocket.
"Come on, little dog," she said. "Would you
like this?" She put the treat behind her, then
went back to scratching Foxie.

Preacher crawled behind Kiarna. He
grabbed the treat and backed off.

"There's another one if you want it," said

Kiarna. She laid a treat next to her.

My junior Jack licked his chops and looked at me.

"Get the treat before Foxie does, Preacher," I said. "Kiarna is *good*. So are lots of other children."

Preacher came closer. This time, he ate the treat before backing away. Kiarna offered a small piece of cheese. Preacher gave her fingers a quick lick, and Kiarna giggled. Preacher's tail came up.

Red gave Kiarna a nudge with his nose. "Chase me!" he said, and bounced away. Kiarna took Foxie off her lap, stood up, then ran off after Red. Blue and Foxie followed, and, after a moment, so did my junior Jack. Pawfect!

I wanted to play too, but of paws I didn't. I had a ham to guard.

Jack's Glossary

Alpha. *The pack leader. A pack leader may be a dog or a human.*

Ig-gnawed. *Ignored, but done by dogs.*

Terrier-tory. *A territory belonging to a terrier.*

Pawsuit. *Pursuit, for dogs.*

Hen-sterics. *Like hysterics. Noisy silliness from hens.*

Pan-dog-monium. *A lot of noise that involves dogs.*

Interrier-gate. *Official questioning, done by a terrier.*

Terrier-fied. *Terrified, for terriers.*

Hangdog. *Miserable, with tail hanging low.*

Comings and Goings

Kiarna and Uncle Smith had supper with us, but I kept up my doggo obbo. It was pawfully difficult to keep track of all the comings and goings. The Boots' van came

back, and Sarge talked to Brown Boots about tents. Shiny Boots and Old Boots loaded boxes and chairs into the van. Old Boots chattered away, but Shiny Boots just grumbled. Auntie Tidge and Caterina Smith came over to our place.

Red dashed back and forth, wanting Kiarna to play. Preacher dashed with him.

Then Jill Russell slunk into Foxie's yard. That seemed odd. Jill isn't the sort of dog who slinks. I watched her creep to Foxie's dogdoor and poke her nose through. She sniff-sniffed.

I darted up and poked her with my nose. "Are you trying to heist that ham, Jill?"

Jill Jack-jumped backwards. "Of paws!" she snapped. "We need a case for Preacher."

"Preacher's happy playing with Kiarna," I said.

Jill sniff-sniffed greedily. "But—"

I sighed. "Do you *want* to get shut in the shed during the wedding feast?"

Auntie Tidge and Caterina came back, and later Caterina and Uncle Smith went to Uptown House. Kiarna stayed with Auntie Tidge. Preacher ran back with Foxie, and Red and Blue managed to stay behind. The Boots' van came back for another load of chairs. "That's the lot then," called Old Boots, as he drove away again.

It was a busy evening, and finally I went to sleep and dreamed of ham.

When I woke up the next morning, Auntie Tidge had already gone. My junior Jack was missing from our yard. I thought he was probably with Kiarna. But where was Kiarna? Where was Sarge? Where was Foxie?

I made a nose map.

Jack's map:

1. Whole huge ham.

2. Lots of people.

3. Lots of dogs.

I **sneefled** to clear my nose. The scent was confused because our street had been so crowded. Sarge wasn't home. Neither was Foxie, so I sniff-sniffed outside our yard.

I detected Jill Russell, Foxie, Auntie Tidge, the three Boots, Sarge, Caterina, Kiarna, Preacher, Red, Blue, Polly and Gloria Smote. I sneefled again. This was **im-paw-sible**.

Think, Jack, I told myself. *Choose one scent to track.* I tried, but most trails ended where people or dogs had gotten into cars.

I tracked Jill Russell to the station. She wasn't pleased to see me. "I didn't heist that ham," she growled.

"No one heisted the ham," I agreed. "It's safe in Auntie Tidge's pantry."

I was helping Jill eat kibble when the Boots' van went past again, heading for my place.

Jill sniff-sniffed after it. "I can still smell that whole huge ham, all the way from Auntie Tidge's place."

So could I.

"Let's go and make sure no one's heisting it," suggested Jill.

"No, let's go to Uptown House," I said. "Then *you* won't be tempted to heist it."

Jill lifted her lip at me, but she came along. We went through the park and scooted up the hill.

"Jack!" Lord Red raced to meet me. "There's lots going on here." He whirled and galloped back to his yard.

He was right. There was lots going on at Uptown House. Auntie Tidge and her friends were in the kitchen preparing for the next day's wedding feast. I saw Sarge and Brown Boots, Old Boots, Walter Barkley and Uncle Smith setting out chairs. Kitty Booker and Caterina sorted buckets of flowers.

Foxie and Blue were playing ball with Kiarna. Preacher dashed to join in, yapping. Kitty Booker put down her bucket. "Isn't Sarge's younger dog afraid of children? We had some trouble up at the library."

Caterina laughed. "All the dogs love Kiarna. I think she's cured him."

The Boots' van came back. Sarge went down to the station. Jack Johnson came back with him. Jill greeted him. Uncle Smith called to Blue. The **terrier-phone** rang in the kitchen. Red ran inside and ouched his tail in the dogdoor.

Jill and I watched the comings and goings.

Jack's Facts

All dogs are observant.
Jack Russells are more observant than most.
Not even a Jack Russell can observe and consider every coming and every going, and I missed an im-paw-tant one.
This is a fact.

Jack's Glossary

Sneefle. *A snorting sneeze, done to clear the nose.*

Im-paw-sible. *Impossible, for dogs.*

Terrier-phone. *A thing that rings.*

Means, Motive and Op-Paw-Tunity

At last, we went home. Sarge took Foxie, Uncle Smith, Blue and me. Auntie Tidge said she'd bring Kiarna and Preacher. As I jumped out at our gate, I knew something was wrong.

I sniff-sniffed around our fence, in case a strange dog had been on my terrier-tory without **pawmission**. I couldn't detect one, but still, something was *wrong*.

I couldn't smell a new scent, but an *old* scent was missing.

People. Dogs. Hens. *Check.*

Fat Molly. Cars. Vans. *Check.*

Kibble. Foxie's old boot. *Check.*

Ham? No. The ham scent had faded almost away.

Someone had heisted the whole huge ham.

I couldn't believe it! I'd ordered my pals to leave that ham alone! I turned on Foxie and Blue. "Which of you is the pupetrator?"

Foxie scratched his elbow. "What are you talking about?"

"The ham," I said. "It's been heisted."

"Ham!" yelled Foxie. "Mine, mine, mine . . ." He tore in through his dogdoor.

"It was you!" I accused Blue. "You heisted that ham!"

Blue hackled. "I did not. I—"

"Blue." Uncle Smith collared him. "Mind your manners." I scooted after Foxie.

I found him outside the pantry door, pawing and sniff-sniffing. "Ham! Ham!"

"The ham's gone," I said. "I told you. It's been heisted."

"It can't have been!" **pawsisted** Foxie, still clawing at the door. "I'm the only dog with the right to heist that ham, and I've been at Uptown House all day!"

"Did you nip home for a nibble? You *said* you'd heist it," I reminded him. "You had the motive, and you have **form**."

"But I had no **op-paw-tunity**," snapped Foxie. "*You* could have done it, Jack. You were snoring when the rest of us left this morning."

"I didn't heist the ham," I said. "It was safe when I left."

"Then Jill Russell did it."

"She couldn't have." I told Foxie I'd tracked Jill to the station. "Jill and I both verified the ham from there," I added.

"Jill sneaked back to eat it later," said Foxie. "She could have, and she would have."

"Jill Russell had the motive," I agreed,

"but not the op-paw-tunity. She was with me the whole time."

"Let's face it, Jack Russell," said Foxie. "*Any* dog in Doggeroo had the motive to heist that ham. A lot of them had op-paw-tunities. I was at Uptown House. So was Preacher. Red and Blue were there, and you and Jill Russell. But there are plenty of others."

I thought about that. "We saw Polly and Spotty and Shuffle in their yards on our way to Uptown House."

"They could have nipped here after that," said Foxie. "Or those Squekes might have done it. There are three of them. Or Ralf Boxer."

"Dogwash!" I said. "Never mind motive and op-paw-tunity. What about *means*? That ham is bigger than Ralf and the Squekes. It's too heavy for a small dog. Even you would have trouble dragging it away."

"I'd manage," snarled Foxie. "I'd bite and nibble until it was small enough to drag."

"That would take all day and leave a drag-trail to follow," I said. "I **dog-duce** the canine criminal is a *big* dog."

"Or a team of small dogs working together," growled Foxie.

I sniff-sniffed carefully around the kitchen. My super-sniffer detected my tracks, Foxie's, and Preacher's. Red's, Blue's, and Jill's were there too. I sneefled crossly. We'd *all* been in the kitchen recently. "I can't scent the Squekes or Ralf," I told Foxie.

"It was Red. Or Blue. Or both of them," he said. "They're big dogs. They have means."

I remembered something. "What about the pantry door? No dog could open that."

"Auntie Tidge took it then," snarled Foxie. "She's the ham heister."

Of paws! Auntie Tidge put the ham in the pantry. She could take it out again. Case closed. But when had she taken it? She'd been at Uptown House all day.

We were chewing over the problem when Auntie Tidge came in with Kiarna and Preacher. "Yes, dear, you can have **special biscuits** for Preacher," said Auntie Tidge. "I'll get them from the pantry." She looked at us and tutted. "You dogs aren't *still* after that ham? You know you'll get some trimmings."

Kiarna giggled. "They're funny, Auntie Tidge. I'm so glad Auntie Caterina is marrying Sarge. Now you and Jack and Preacher will be part of my family."

Auntie Tidge laughed. "Keep the dogs back while I get the biscuits, dear, otherwise they'll be after the ham."

Kiarna cuddled us all while Auntie Tidge went into the pantry. We heard her open the

biscuit box. Then she said, "That's funny."

"What is?" Kiarna asked, scratching my neck.

"Someone's taken the ham," said Auntie Tidge.

Auntie Tidge checked with Sarge, Uncle Smith and Caterina. None of them had taken the ham from the pantry. Next, she called Brown Boots on the terrier-phone.

"Well, Auntie?" asked Sarge, when she

hung up.

Auntie Tidge sighed. "He and his helpers took the other things to Uptown House yesterday. He says they left the ham and the big cake as I instructed. Today they were putting up the tent and setting out chairs, remember? I don't understand. Why would anyone take a ham?"

Jack's Facts

Auntie Tidge is an intelligent person.
Even intelligent people sometimes don't see the obvious.
This is a fact.

Like any dog, I knew *why* someone would heist a ham. What I didn't know was who, or where, or how!

Auntie Tidge ordered a new ham from Butcher Beale. "But please don't deliver it until tomorrow after the wedding," she said. "I don't want another one going missing."

Jack's Glossary

Pawmission. *Permission, given by a dog.*

Pawsisted. *Kept doggedly on.*

Form. *If a dog has form, he has been a canine criminal in an earlier case.*

Op-paw-tunity. *Opportunity, for dogs.*

Dog-duce. *Deduce, or figure out using logic.*

Special biscuits. *Auntie Tidge makes these. They don't harm terrier teeth.*

Su-paw-rior Reasoning

The next morning, we went back to Uptown House. On the way, my super-sniffer detected no whiff of ham. I tried to interrier-gate Red, but he was playing with Kiarna.

I was baffled. Every dog in Doggeroo had motive. A few had op-paw-tunity. None had means. Smaller dogs couldn't open the pantry, or drag the ham. Bigger dogs could carry the ham, but couldn't open the pantry. *Really* big dogs might break the pantry door and carry the ham, but couldn't get through Foxie's dogdoor.

"It all points in one direction," I told Foxie. *"Teamwork."*

"The Squekes!" said Foxie.

"They couldn't open the door, Uncle Foxie," said Preacher. "And there was no Squeke-scent in the kitchen. I think **pawhaps** it was a dog and a human working together. The dog has motive and op-paw-tunity. The human has means."

"That was **su-paw-rior** reasoning," I told him. I was proud of my junior Jack.

"The blue stealer has form with a bad human," reminded Foxie.

"Blue is a good dog now, and *that* human isn't in Doggeroo," I said. "It could have been Red and Caterina, but Caterina wouldn't heist the ham. She'll get plenty at her wedding feast. Besides, Red was *here*."

"Maybe it was Blue and Uncle Smith," said Foxie. "They both admired that ham."

"Dogwash!" I said. "They were here at

Uptown House when Jill and I arrived. They didn't leave until after the ham was heisted."

"It was the Boots and Ralf Boxer, then," said Foxie.

"No Ralf scent in the kitchen, and the Boots were helping Sarge with the tent."

Foxie suggested more im-paw-sible teams of ham heisters. Preacher got bored and ran to play hide-and-squeak with Red and Kiarna. I wanted to join in, but I know my

duty as a dog detective. I continued to chew over the case.

By now Blue and Jill Russell were in the game. Kiarna was laughing, pouncing out of the bushes to tickle ears, then dashing past Foxie and me, followed by my pals. Then Foxie joined the game. I watched the pattern they made as they all zipped by.

Red, Blue, Kiarna, Preacher, Jill, Foxie.

Red, Blue, Kiarna, Preacher, Jill, Foxie.

Red, Blue, Kiarna, Jill, Foxie.

Red, Blue, Kiarna, Jill, Foxie.

Suddenly, I sat up. Where had Preacher gone?

I was about to track down my junior Jack when he rushed around the corner. "Dad! Dad! Come and see what I detected!"

I followed him around the house and caught up with him in the new greenhouse.

"What have you detected?" I asked. "Mice? Sparrows?"

"Better than that!" Preacher waggled his tail. "I've found the heisted ham!"

Jack's Glossary

Pawhaps. *Perhaps.*

Su-paw-rior. *Superior, the way Jack Russells are.*

Ham-bush

I could hardly believe it. I am an experienced dog detective, and *I* hadn't detected the ham. I sniff-sniffed and picked up a faint whiff of ham. But the whole huge ham should smell stronger than this. Had Preacher found a stray slice from someone's sandwich?

My junior Jack led me proudly to the back of the greenhouse. "I came in to do what dogs do," he reported. "Then I nose-mapped to find Kiarna so I could pounce and surprise her. And guess what? There was ham on my map!"

Preacher's map:

1. Kiarna.

2. Mum Russell.

3. Dad's pals.

4. Lots of people.

5. Ham.

6. Shiny Boots.

He pointed to a big plastic **hamper** tucked under a trailing tomato plant. The lid fitted so tightly only a faint whiff of scent leaked out.

"Very well done, Preacher!" I told my junior Jack. "This is excellent detective work. You really have found the heisted ham."

Preacher waggled his tail. "But who is the pupetrator?" he asked.

I sniff-sniffed the hamper. The ham heister's scent hung around the handle. Now I knew the ham heister wasn't Blue, or Jill, or Foxie, or any of my other suspects. It was a human, working alone! And now that I knew *who*, I also knew *when* and *how*.

When Jill and I had been eating kibble at the station, we'd seen the Boots' van drive past. Brown Boots and Old Boots had been helping Sarge with the tent, but *Shiny Boots* had not been with them. Shiny Boots had taken the van to heist the ham! And not even I had really noticed one more coming and going among so many. But now my super-sniffer had verified the ham heister beyond a doubt.

If Shiny Boots had been a canine criminal, I would have made an arrest. But dog detectives need human help to arrest a human. And Sarge was busy getting ready for his wedding. And Auntie Tidge had ordered a new ham for the feast.

That's when I had a sudden **delicious idea**.

"Preacher," I said. "Call a **council-of-paw**. We need to set up a **ham-bush** and arrange a pan-dog-monium with the **Jack-pack**."

If Kiarna had still been leading the game, arranging the ham-bush would have been difficult. **Paw-tunately**, Auntie Tidge called her to get ready for the wedding.

I gave directions to the Jack-pack and we took up our positions. We lurked and crouched and **lay doggo**. Foxie, Preacher and I hid among the tomato plants. The others pretended to snooze on the path and under the trees outside.

In the front garden, people gathered near the tent. Caterina, Sarge and Kiarna and Sarge's brother came out in special clothes,

and music started to play. The wedding was about to begin.

"We'll miss the wedding feast," grumbled Foxie.

"This case will have an **excellent outcome**," I promised. I jumped up to greet my mother, Ace, who had arrived with Sarge's brother and Dr. Jeanie. She had brought Barley, little Painter and Trump, Jackie and Wednesday. I explained our ham-bush and they all took their places.

It was quiet in the greenhouse, but soon we heard footsteps crunch along the path. Shiny Boots was coming back to collect his booty.

We lay doggo as he bent over the hamper. The lock clicked as he removed the lid. "Yum!" he said. "*Ham!*" He reached into the hamper and hoisted out the whole huge ham.

I gave the signal for the ham-bush to be sprung.

Preacher and I burst from the tomato plants with the loudest Jack-yaps ever yapped by Jacks. Foxie yammered and bounced and hollered, "Ham, *ham,* HAM!" The rest of the Jack-pack tore in from outside, yelping, yapping and baying.

The ham-bush worked pawfectly.

Shiny Boots yelled with shock and dropped the whole huge ham. He ran away as fast as his boots could go. Of paws we didn't run off in pawsuit. The heisted ham had *hit the ground.* We had im-paw-tant salvage to consider.

Jack's Facts

Food that hits the ground automatically belongs to dogs.

Therefore, it is not stealing to eat this food.
In fact, it is salvage and salvage has to
be eaten.
This is a fact.

Jack's Glossary

Hamper. *A box that should hold ham.*

Delicious idea. *The kind of idea that leads to a feast for deserving dog detectives.*

Council-of-paw. *Council of war, especially for dogs.*

Ham-bush. *Laying a trap and springing out to scare a ham heister into dropping the ham.*

Jack-pack. *A noble pack of dogs united under a strong leader.*

Paw-tunately. *Fortunately.*

Lay doggo. *Kept quiet so as not to be detected.*

Excellent outcome. *The end of a case that pleases almost everyone, especially the dog detective.*

Epi-dog

Shiny Boots never confessed to being a
heister. We must have taught him a lesson
though, because he helped clean up after
the wedding feast. Auntie Tidge gave him
lots of ham sandwiches. She never found
out what happened to the whole huge ham.

Everyone enjoyed the wedding feast.
Sarge and Caterina pranced. So did Auntie
Tidge and Uncle Smith, and all our favorite
people. Kiarna played find-the-treat with Red
and Preacher.

The new ham smelled almost as good as
the old one. It probably tasted as good too,

but I can't say for sure. For some reason, I didn't feel like salvaging even a nibble.

It's paw-sible the ham heist was my **best case ever**.

Jack's Glossary

Best case ever. *The kind of case that begins and ends with ham.*

About the Authors

Darrel and Sally Odgers live in Tasmania with their Jack Russell terriers, Tess, Trump, Pipwen, Jeanie and Preacher, who compete to take them for walks. They enjoy walks, because that's when they plan their stories. They toss ideas around and pick the best. They are also the authors of the popular *Pet Vet* series.

PET VET The new series from the authors of Jack Russell: Dog Detective!

Meet Trump! She's an A.L.O., or Animal Liaison Officer. She works with Dr. Jeanie, the young vet who runs Pet Vet Clinic in the country town of Cowfork. Dr. Jeanie looks after animals that are sick or injured. She also explains things to the owners. But what about the animals? Who will tell them what's going on? That's where Trump comes in.

JACK RUSSELL:
Dog Detective

Read all of Jack's adventures!

Jack Russell:
the detective with
a nose for crime.